AN
HISTORICAL AND DESCRIPTIVE
GUIDE
TO THE TOWN OF
WIMBORNE MINSTER,
DORSETSHIRE;

WITH A
PARTICULAR ACCOUNT OF THE COLLEGIATE CHURCH OF
St. Cuthberge,
QUEEN ELIZABETH'S FREE GRAMMAR
School,
THE CHAPEL OF ST. MARGARET,
AND
OTHER CHARITABLE ENDOWMENTS IN THE SAME PARISH.

Second Edition.

WIMBORNE:
ALFRED PURKIS, CHURCH STREET.
LONDON: LONGMAN, BROWN, GREEN, AND CO.
M.DCCC.LIII.

ADVERTISEMENT
TO THE FIRST EDITION.

THE following pages have been written and compiled under the idea that a town so ancient and venerable, and once so wealthy and important, as Wimborne Minster, was entitled to more minute attention than it has hitherto received from the generality of its visitors and inhabitants. Should the sketch now offered tend in any degree to promote the fulfilment of this object, the wishes of the author will be attained. It has not been hastily put together, or without a careful reference to the best sources of information; while the descriptive matter has been prepared from personal and repeated investigations. The ground-work of that portion, in which the present condition of the Minster-Church is depicted, originally appeared in the first volume of "The Crypt," a periodical journal, devoted more particularly to the illustration of the antiquities and literature of the West. For the remainder, the elaborate and expensive County History, by Hutchins, has furnished the principal materials, though not without the aid of other authorities of less obvious celebrity. The list of charitable benefactions, in particular, has been revised and corrected by comparison with other extracts from the papers of the late Mr. Nicholas Russell. Such as it is, the work is now presented to the public in a form as unostentatious, and at a price as reasonable, as could be devised, consistently with the needful illustrations, in a humble hope that some service may thus be rendered to readers of every class, in a department of study too frequently confined to the exclusive gratification of the wealthy.

PREFACE.

The former edition of Mr. Hall's Guide to the town having been long since exhausted, and the want of a concise History of the Town and Neighbourhood being much felt, it has been thought desirable to bring out another edition of the Work, with various corrections. Much additional matter will also be found, relating to the history of the town.

Independently of the advantages derived from being surrounded by a fertile neighbourhood, the town has for many years enjoyed the benefit of the Free Grammar School of Queen Elizabeth,—which was for a long series of years conducted by the late Rev. J. Mayo, a man whose kindness of disposition and generosity of heart, will cause him long to be remembered.—A new scheme having been adopted for the administration of the charity, the School-house has been rebuilt, and additional masters engaged. Such information has been now introduced in the following pages, as would be sought for by those wishing to obtain the advantages of an education in this Royal Foundation School.

LIST OF THE SUBSCRIBERS.

Adey, Stanworth, Esq., London,
Atherton, Mrs. Col., Wimborne.
Austen, Rev. J. H., Ensbury.
Bailey, J., Esq., Wimborne, two copies.
Bartlett, Henry, Esq., Wimborne.
Bartlett, Mr. S., New Barn, Wimborne.
Belben, George, Jun., Esq., Poole.
Bernard Rev. —
Blount, Mr. F. S., Wimborne
Blount, Mr. H. S., Wimborne.
Brown, Mr. R. Canford.
Bryant, Isaac, Esq., Wimborne.
Burne, Mr. W., Poole, two copies.
Burt, Mr., Wimborne.
Carnegie, Miss, Wimborne.
Carnegie, J., Esq., M.D., Wimborne.
Case, Rev. T., Horton.
Castleman, Henry, Esq., Beech House, two copies.
Clarke, Mr. A., Wimborne, two copies.
Clinch, Mrs., London.
Coffin, Mr. I. W., Wimborne.
Coombs, I., Esq., Dorchester.

Couch, Miss, Gillscott, Devon.
Croom, James, Esq., Blandford.
Dew, Mr. W., Wimborne.
Dew, Mr. I., Wimborne.
Druitt, Miss, the Square, Wimborne.
Druitt, Miss J., Wimborne.
Druitt, W., Esq., Wimborne.
Dyke, Mr. Charles, Wimborne.
Ellis, Mr. Charles, Junr., Wimborne.
Eyers, Miss, Wimborne.
Falmouth, the Countess of, two copies.
Fletcher, Rev. W., D.D., Wimborne.
Frampton, Mr. H., Wimborne, two copies.
Freeman, F. W., Esq., Wimborne.
Fryer, Mr. J., Junr., Wimborne.
Garland, John, Esq., Dorchester.
Godber, Mr.
Greathead, Miss
Guest, Lady Charlotte, Canford House, twelve copies.
Gray, Mr. John, Wimborne.
Hall, Rev. Edward.
Harris, George, Esq., Henbury House, two copies.
Hart, Miss, Wimborne.
Harvey, J., Esq., Hemsworth.
Hatchard, Mrs., Hill Butts.
Hawes, R., Esq., Wimborne.
Hawke, Mr., Wimborne.
Hayter, Mr. T., Wimborne.
Hayter, Mr. H., Wimborne.

Henning, Mr. Edward, Wimborne, two copies.
Hill, Isaac, Esq., Wimborne.
Hopkins, Mr., Wimborne.
Hopkins, Mr. Robert, Wimborne.
Hoskins, Mr. George, Burton on Trent.
Howel, Miss, Weymouth.
Irving, Master
Kemp, Mr. W., Hill Butts.
Kent, Mr. H., Wimborne.
Knott, Mr. J., Wimborne.
Langer, Mr. W., Wimborne.
Lewer, Mrs. Edward, Wimborne.
Lewer, Mr. F. C., Wimborne.
Lewer, R., Esq., King's College, London.
Lewis, Mr. Samuel, Sherborne, two copies.
Linthorne, B., Esq., High Hall.
Ludlow, Mr. A., Wimborne.
Machin, Mr. I., lay vicar, Salisbury,
Mapleton, Mrs., Wimborne.
M'Calmont, Rev. T., Hill Butts, Wimborne, and Highfield, Southampton.
March, Mr. L., Wimborne.
Mayo, Miss, Wimborne, three copies.
Mayo, Thomas, Esq.
Moore, H., Esq., Wimborne.
Morgan, Mr. C. H., Salisbury.
Müller, Mrs., Farrs, near Wimborne.
Okeden, W. P., Esq.
Oxford, Mr. A., Wimborne.

Patey, George E., Esq., Canford.
Pearce, Mr. James, London.
Phillips, R. A. L., Esq., Wimborne.
Pitt, Mr. W., Wimborne.
Pope, Mrs.
Pratt, Mr., Oxford.
Purkis, Mrs., Weymouth.
Purkis, Mr. H., Brunswick Place, Southampton.
Pyne, J., Esq., Canford.
Reeves, Mr. John, Fordingbridge.
Rooke, Master.
Rowe, E. H., Esq., Wimborne.
Score, Mr. John, Wimborne.
Scott, Rev. Charles, Wimborne.
Scott, Mr. J. Hill, Wimborne.
Solly, E. Esq., London, two copies.
Spink, Rev. S., Dover.
Tatum, Mr. G. R., Salisbury.
Toppin, Mr. P.
Webb, Mr. W. G., Wimborne.
Woodbridge, Mr. H. W.
Vey, Mr. J., Wimborne.
Evans, G., Esq., Wimborne.

	PAGE
EARLY History of Wimborne	1
The Nunnery	3
The Deanery	4
The Exterior of the Minster Church	6
Interior of the same	11
The Organ	17
The Churchyard	31
Altars, Furniture, and Relics of the Church	33
Ecclesiastical arrangements	35
Queen Elizabeth's Grammar School	36
Clergymen, Masters of the School, &c.	41
Independent Chapel	42
Wesleyan Chapel	47
National School	47
British School, Mechanics' Institution	48
St Margaret's Hospital, and other Charities	49
The Town	51
Badbury Rings	52
Stapehill Nunnery	53
Country Seats	54
Nineveh Marbles at Canford House	57

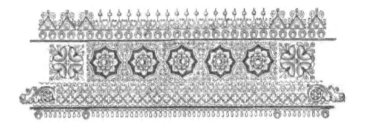

A Guide

TO

WIMBORNE MINSTER.

WIMBORNE MINSTER is a parish and market-town of great antiquity, in Badbury Hundred, Shaftesbury Division, Dorsetshire. It is situated upon a dry, gravelly soil, in a fertile and delightful vale, upon the Allen, near its confluence with the Stour, with a bridge over either river. It is distant from London 100 miles, S. W.; from Poole, 6 miles, N.; from Blandford, 10 miles, S. E.; and from Dorchester, 22 miles, N. E.

Its Roman apellation, according to Antonine's Itinerary, was *Vindogladia*; in that of Richard of Cirencester it is written *Ventageladia*; and in the Geography of Ravennas, *Bindogladia*. The Saxon word, *Wimbourns*, is supposed to have been derived from *Win*, the ancient name of the

Allen, now familiarly termed *the Brook*, which flows on the North and East sides of the town; and *Bourne*, a rivulet; *Win* also signifies *a battle*. Simeon of Durham, and Henry of Huntingdon, Historians of the seventh century, write it *Winburnham: Ham* signifying *a habitation*. The addition of *Minster* is used to distinguish this place, as the seat of the Collegiate or Monastic Church, from Wimbourne All Saints', and Wimbourne St. Giles', in the same county. Tanner christens it *Twin-born*, and derives the appellation from the junction of its sister rivers.

Wimbourne-Minster is recorded as a town of note and importance, even under the dominion of the Romans; who made it the winter camp, or head-quarters, to their summer station at Badbury Rings. By the Saxons it was certainly considered of consequence; and Camden says that, in their time, it was strongly fortified, and still retained an air of Roman decoration. Yet some persons have conjectured that Badbury itself was the Roman Vindogladia, and that the Saxons first descended into Wimbourne about the seventh century, from the same dislike to high winds and military interruptions which induced their posterity, six hundred years afterwards, to desert the bulwarks of Old Sarum for the more sheltered retreats of Salisbury.

In the year 901, we find this neighbourhood the scene of several contests. Edward the Elder, first son of Alfred the Great, and seventh monarch of the Saxons, was opposed in his hereditary rights by Ethelwold, his cousin-germain. The latter seized upon Christchurch and Wimborne; but being routed, after considerable resistance, by Edward, who lay encamped at Badbury, he first, according to Higden's Polychronicon, restored his wife, whom he had carried off from Wimborne Nunnery, and then took refuge with the Danes of Northumberland. By them he was acknowledged King of England; but, unable to withstand the pursuit of his adversaries, he retreated into Normandy.

Landing, however, a few years afterwards, in Essex, he was encountered by his brother in a pitched battle, near Bury St. Edmund's, his followers dispersed, and himself, with many eminent commanders, slain upon the spot.

THE NUNNERY, just alluded to, was among the earliest houses of the kind in this country. It was founded by Cuthberga, or Lutleberga, daughter of Kenred, and sister of Ina, both Kings of the West Saxons. This lady, about the year 705, had been espoused to Egfrid, King of Northumberland; but discarding her husband before the day of nuptials, she retired to the monastery of Barking, in Essex. Returning from thence, about 713, she commenced a similar institution at Wimborne, which was probably completed within ten years. Here she spent the remainder of her days in devotion, and, in 727, was interred, as Leland informs us, in the Presbytery of the Church, where her memory was yearly celebrated on the last day of August. Quinburga, her sister, is by some supposed to have been buried with her.

The Nunnery, having fallen a prey to the incursions of the Danes, was succeeded by a DEANERY, OR COLLEGE OF SECULAR CANONS; though Butler, in his Lives of the Saints, considers the Nunnery and the College to have existed at the same time. This restoration is assigned to Edward the Confessor; who amply endowed his new foundation, and furnished it with a Dean, four Prebendaries, three Vicars, four Deacons, and five Singers. The College, though spared by Henry in reverence to the benefactions of his grandmother, was dissolved, and its revenues vested in the crown, in the first year of Edward VI. (1547.)[*] These revenues had been valued at near £140 a year, and were now granted, for the most part, to Edward Duke of Somerset; afterwards to Edward Baron Clinton. The remaining portion was made over, with considerable additions, to the Corporation of the College by Queen Elizabeth; though with the reservation of an annual rent to the crown, which was remitted, as well as the grant confirmed, by James the First.

Out of this income, besides the re-endowment of an ancient Grammar School, it was ordained that three Priests and three Clerks should be provided for the perpetual service of the Church and parish, under the regulation of twelve Governors, to be chosen from the most " discreet and substantial " inhabitants of the town, and subject to the Visitation of the Lord Bishop of Bristol.

Disputes, however, arising towards the middle of the reign of Charles the First, between the Governors and the rest of the Parishioners, Archbishop Laud instigated the former to surrender up their charter to the King; who, in consideration of a gift of £1000, re-granted, by a new

---

[*] The famous Reginald Pole, afterwards Cardinal, and Archbishop of Canterbury, was appointed Dean of Wimborne in the year 1517.

patent, all the possessions of the Church and School to a similar body corporate of twelve Governors, but with some accession to the nature and extent of their authority, and stipulations for the maintenance of four choristers, two singing-men, and an organist. Since that time the ordinary expenses of the Church and School have been regularly defrayed at a cost of about £500 a year.*

Of the present CHURCH, OR MINSTER, a most ancient and venerable structure, some idea may be derived from a general view, taken from the N. W. entrance to the Churchyard, and prefixed as a frontispiece to our GUIDE. By Gilpin it is pronounced a specimen of the heaviest and earliest style of Saxon architecture: but we have in fact no ecclesiastical remains in this country, near so considerable in grandeur or extent, of an age precedent to the Conquest. From that period to the end of Richard the First (1066 to 1199) is the great age of Anglo-Norman art. The three next reigns (1200 to 1307) are remarkable for the struggle between that and the lighter style of Gothic, which passed the usual routine of improvement, perfection, and degeneracy, till its final extinction in the middle of the sixteenth century.

Bishop Tanner records that this edifice was originally dedicated to the Virgin Mary; perhaps conjointly to her and to St. Cuthberge; for the honour has been generally appropriated to the latter. Its shape is that of a cross, 180 feet in length, and is divided, like a Cathedral, into

---

* The Act of Parliament more recently passed for the better regulation of Charities, has caused this sum to be greatly augmented. The Tithes being now valued under the Tithe Commutation Act, at £2500.

chancel and choir, with aisles and crypt, transepts, nave, and long-aisles. The exterior presents us with two towers, one in the centre, and one at the west-end, and three porches. From the summit of the centre tower formerly arose a Norman spire, vulgarly recorded to have equalled that of Salisbury in height, and still preserved on the corporation seal, which appears (fig. 1.) with those of the dean (fig. 2.) and the official (fig. 3.) on the accompanying plate.* This spire, from the continual concussion of the bells, at length gave way, and left the greater part of the choir in ruins.

"Having discoursed thus longe of this Church," says Mr. Coker, in his survey of Dorsetshire, "I will not overpasse a strange accident, which in our dayes happened unto it: viz. *Anno Domini*, 1600, (the Choire beeing then full of people at tenne of clock Service, allsoe the streets by reason of the markett:) a sudden mist ariseing, all the Spire Steeple, beeing of a very great height, was strangelie cast downe, the stones battered all the lead, and brake much of the timber of the roofe of the Church, yet without anie hurt to the people: which ruine is sithence commendablie repaired with the Church revenues; for sacriledge hath not yet swept awaye all: beeing assisted by Sir John Hanham, a neighbour Gentleman, who, if I mistake not, enjoyeth revenues of the Church, and hath done commendablie to convert parte of it to its former use." (p. 113-4.)

At the height of some forty feet from the ground, and at

---

* These seals are all in brass, and of the exact size of the engravings. That of the Deanery was recently picked up at Old Castle, near Salisbury, and is now in the possession of the family of the late Sir James Hanham, Bart.

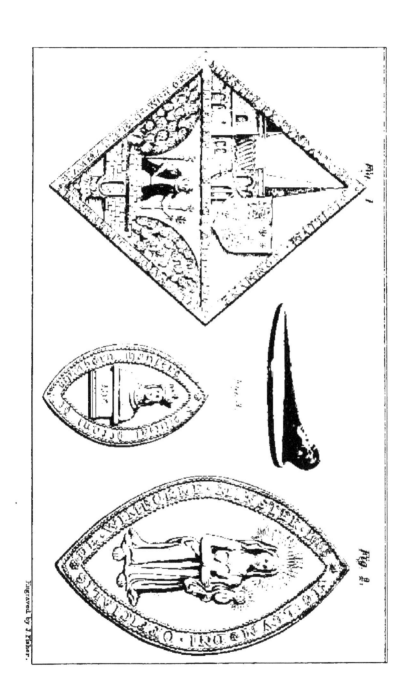

the intersection of the nave and transepts, the first story of the original tower exhibits its three Norman windows; that in the centre, of the earliest pointed arch; that on either side, of the still more ancient circular, with its clustered shafts and rudely sculptured capitals, betraying occasionally the intermediate stages between debased Corinthian and the first dawn of Gothic. The two last-mentioned are now entirely open; the lower halves were until recently blocked up, and only the upper portions employed as windows: the middle arch does not appear to have been ever pierced for that purpose. The second story consists of seven round arches, of the same size with those below, intersecting one another; and, what is remarkable, the pointed arches formed by this intersection are marked out, apparently for better observation, by a bold and distinct cornice. These arches, of which only one intersection has been opened to admit light and air into the tower, present probably one of the earliest specimens in England of the genuine pointed Gothic; and, with their chaplet of small heads and beam-ends above, beautifully executed and excellently preserved, the whole variegated by the mellow tints of red or iron-stone, and by a sombre ivy just creeping round from the opposite side, form a very beautiful and interesting feature. The four angles of the tower are gracefully broken by a slender shaft, which is here surmounted by a projecting head. But of a very inferior style is all above: the heavy parapet and clumsy pinnacles betray the deterioration of science under the auspices of the House of Stuart.

Turning away from the north transept window, which is large but unsightly, and pausing but a few moments to notice the old turret which leads to the *triforium*, or gallery of the nave, and to the tower-lantern, let us survey the principal porch with its ample door-way, its pediment pitched so high as to form an acute triangle, (within which is situated the *muniment*, or record *room*,) and its low narrow buttresses at the corners. We may then wind round the other tower on the right into the south side of the church-yard, carefully avoiding to look up as we pass the western extremity, lest we encounter to our cost that exquisite effort of *church-warden architecture*, still extant from the year 1739, in a huge oval window, inserted within the outline of its Gothic predecessor, now plaistered up, together with a pigmy kettle headed-portal, superinscribed with the names and styles of its dignified designers. On proceeding further, however, we shall find the general effects of this tower from a distance by no means displeasing.

The pinnacles, it is true, are disproportionably small, a fault not unusual in Gothic buildings of the fifteenth century; but with this drawback, the whole rises gracefully to the height of about 100 feet from the ground, as was the custom of the age, and its details are for the most part simple and correct. The stone of which it is composed was granted in the year 1448, by Sir John Benton, Lord of the Manor of Hampreston; but the work was not completed till sixteen years afterwards. Within, is a peal of six old and capital bells removed hither from the chapel of Kingston; upon which the chimes are performed every quarter of an hour, by a figure dressed as a verger, or wearing canonicals, who stands with his hammers in front of one of the northern windows; until recently this post was occupied by a soldier, who stood accoutred cap-a-pie, but the former figure being deemed more in character with the building was substituted for the soldier. The great bell, originally dedicated to St. Cuthberge, and called after her name, was re-cast in 1629; it weighs 36½ cwt., and bears round the rim the following memorial: "Mr. Willielmus Loringe me primo fecit in honorem Sanctæ Cuthbergæ: renovabar sumptu parochiali per A. B. anno Domini, 1629."

The south porch still bears the relic of its stone cross, and the holy emblem of the lamb, sculptured in relief: while the older tower here appears even more elegant than before, and the line of quaint *gargoyles*, or water-spouts, projecting from the nave, gives an additional variety to the outline. The round turret in the south transept, containing a staircase to the library, is superior to that on the opposite side by the addition of a *finial*, or tuft of flowers, and a circle of minute battlements. But instead of dwelling on the abomination of a square painted dial aloft, let us examine the two ancient grave-stones, or coffins, at our feet. They bear no legible inscription, nor are they handed down by any authentic account; but tradition reports, that two officers of rank, in the days of chivalry, having been guilty of some offence against the romantic spirit of the period, flung themselves from off the summit of the spire, rather than encounter the disgrace of a judicial atonement, and were here interred, where they fell, side by side.

(Tombstones of this shape and character are not usually found in churchyards. But it is well known that a Church, dedicated to St. Mary, stood, within the last ninety years, in the square of the present market-place: its ruins, indeed, as well as those of the Cross, and the Town Hall adjacent, were in the memory of persons who but a few years ago lived in their vicinity; and a dwellinghouse, now church-property, and occupying the same spot, continues to be entered as *St. Mary's* in the account books of the Church-wardens. The figure of the Knight Templar, hereafter noticed in the Choir-Aisle, was unquestionably removed to its present site on the demolition of St. Mary's in the Market; and it seems by no means improbable that both the remains of Ethelred, and the stone coffins in the burial-ground, may have been also taken from this or some other ecclesiastical building in the town, now no longer in existence.)

In a survey, thus far, of the exterior of the church, abundant traces will be observed of an innovation, though not a very recent one, from which almost every Gothic edifice in this country appears to have more or less suffered. This is, a contraction in the height of the roof, by which a few pounds have been saved in the expense of lead or slates, (the latter, by the way, a paltry substitute for the grey and mossy stone,) at the same time that an awkward mark is left on the outside, ornaments and windows are demolished or concealed within, and of course the proportions of the building materially altered.

But there will be more to notice upon this point, when we enter. Meanwhile, in passing the east end of the choir,

EASTERN, OR ALTAR, WINDOW OF WIMBORNE MINSTER CHURCH.

those who are acquainted with the interior aspect of the great window, will not fail to look up for a corresponding effect from the outside; and will to equal certainty be disappointed at its insignificance. The arches below appear to have formerly enlightened the crypt; but the curtailments of the latter have both rendered useless, and at the same time effectually stopped up the former.

We are now on the north once more, and have well nigh completed our circuit. But can we gain admittance only by this incongruous porch, the wretched masonry of 1714? Let it not be told, that this very door was once a window, now indeed wedged up within the cumbrous pile, yet not so effectually hidden, but that he who traverses the north aisle may discover the injury inflicted. Fortunately, here is an old fashioned little door-way by its side, through which we may suppose that penitents were formerly dismissed after confession, and by which we may enter at our leisure.

THE CHOIR exhibits at this time so little of its original beauty, that the visitor's attention immediately settles upon almost the only remain that can be dignified with the title of magnificent. The east window over the altar, (represented in the opposite engraving,) is equally remarkable for its elegance and its peculiarity. It consists of three distinct *lights*, separated by clustered shafts of Purbeck marble, and each rising up into a lancet form, until, just as it begins to close into a point, it suddenly diverges, and ends in a circular head. The centre light is permounted by a *quatrefoil*, those on each side by a *sexfoil;* round the former runs a moulding of unusual shape, somewhat resembling a hollow lozenge, which with the addition of finials and corbel-heads, is sufficient to constitute a very rich and beautiful window. The stained glass for the centre light, with which the window is ornamented, was given by W. J. Bankes, Esq., and was imported from the Continent; it represents the genealogy of our Saviour, commencing with David. The side lights were executed by Willomet. Beneath the window is the communion table, with a carved oak chair on each side. On the south side of the altar stand three ancient stalls, crowned with lofty finials, whither the officiating ministers retired during those portions of the service performed by the choir, and which are still supplied by chairs in Roman Catholic Chapels of the present day. Beyond these, a similar recess contains the *piscina*, or *stoup*, a kind of sink, where the priest emptied the water with which he had washed his hands, as well as any impurities in the chalice, which were carried down through a pipe into a subterraneous drain. On the opposite side of the altar, on a level with the ground, is fixed a brass plate, representing a king in his robes, with his crown and sceptre: at the bottom is an escutcheon of the same metal, charged with a cross flory, and in the centre, upon another plate, is this inscription:

IN HOC LOCO QUIESCIT CORPUS STI
ETHELREDI, REGIS WEST SAXONUM, MARTYRIS,
QUI ANO. DOM. 873, 23°. DIE APRILIS, PER MANUS
DACORUM PAGANORUM OCCUBUIT.

"In this place reposes the body of St. Ethelred, the

Martyr, King of the West Saxons, who fell by the hands of the Pagan Danes, on the 23rd day of April, in the year of our Lord 873." The centre plate is evidently not of early workmanship: in fact, Roman capitals were not in use till the reign of James the First. Both Leland and Camden mention the *recent repairs* of the tomb, and give the figures 872. But, what is most curious, there is still preserved in the vestry-room another, and probably an older, copy of the *inscription alone*, in *brass*; (for that now inserted is on *copper*, and pared away to fit in between the effigy and the coat of arms;) and the figures upon this plate are 872. But it is further remarkable that each of these dates is wrong: for Ethelred, the elder brother of Alfred, was mortally wounded, probably at Meretun, or Marten, in S. Wilts, in 871; he died immediately afterwards at Wittingham, or Witchampton, in Dorsetshire, and was here interred under a marble monument.

Notwithstanding the dignity conferred upon the high altar of a double ascent of five steps into the choir, and six more into the chancel, a striking deformity arises from the latter being injudiciously brought forward, so that the extent of the raised space is out of all proportion with the limits of the church. It would seem, from the gradations in the seats of the stalls, that they were originally situated *on* the steps, rising one above another, and not on the level pavement of the altar, as they now stand.

At the foot of the altar, and in front of two glazed arches which lead into the side aisles, are two oblong square monuments of grey marble. That on the north bears the following fragment,—all that was spared it is said, in the time of the commonwealth,—of a brass inscription along the verge :

" . . . . . conjux quondam Henrici Courteney, Marchionis Exon, et mater Edwardi Courteney, nuper Ao . . . ."

This tomb was erected for Gertrude, daughter of William Blount, Lord Mountjoy, second wife of Henry Courteney, Marquess of Exeter, and mother of Edward Courteney, last Earl of Devonshire, who died at Padua, in 1556. The husband of this lady was beheaded, with several others, by order of Henry the Eighth, in 1538; she herself was attainted, but pardoned, and died twenty years subsequently. About ninety years ago the tomb was opened, out of wantonness, and the body discovered wrapped in cere-cloth; being placed in an erect posture, the back-bone gave way, and all the other parts fell to pieces. The mutilated condition of the monument may be partly attributed to the same mischievous curiosity. It was again opened in 1839, for the purpose of removing it slightly forward, to admit the handsomely decorated stained glass above, which now fills the arch, and which was executed by command of the Earl of Devon.

The other presents us with the recumbent effigies, in alabaster, of John de Beaufort, brother-in-law of James the First of Scotland, nephew of Cardinal Beaufort, and grandson of 'old John of Gaunt, time-honour'd Lancaster,' created Duke of Somerset in 1443, and deceased the year following; and of Margaret, his wife, daughter of

Sir John Beauchamp, of Bletso, whose only daughter Margaret, Countess of Richmond and Derby, and mother to King Henry the Seventh, erected this monument to her parents, and endowed the free-school of this town. The male figure is in rich and curious armour, a pointed helmet with a coronet on his head, a collar of SS* round his neck, a dagger on his right side, and on his left a sword, of which the hilt alone remains, inscribed with the letters I H S. †
A garter is fastened round his knee; his head is supported by two angels, and his feet by a lion; his left hand holds the gauntlet on his breast, his right clasps that of his wife. She is attired in a long robe of state, with a veil and collar, a coronet on her head, which is supported also by two angels, and at her feet an antelope: in her left hand is a string of beads, a ring on her fore-finger, two others on the second, and two on the third. There are no traces of any escutcheon or inscription; but the soldier's helmet still hangs over his tomb. The arch above is also filled with stained glass, containing heraldic emblazonments of the arms of the Dukes of Beaufort, Somerset, and Richmond, and was placed here at the expense of the Duke of Beaufort. Both these ornaments to the choir were glazed by Willomet.

The windows of the choir, with the single exception before noticed, are insignificant rather than inelegant.

---

* The collar of *Esses*, formed of links in resemblance of that letter, and still worn on certain occasions by our Judges, is by some persons derived from the religious society of St. Simplicius, who was thrown into the Tiber with a chain round his neck by Diocleslan But the more learned agree that this collar was the badge of Henry and the Lancastrian party, in allusion to their watchword, "Souvenez vous de moi," during their meditated overthrow of Richard the Second.

† The old manner of writing this symbol of our Saviour, which occurs in Greek Manuscripts of the New Testament, thus, I H C, with a dash over the

There is one, indeed, over each side of the altar, of a lancet form, with shafts, beautifully purfled throughout; the rest are mean, and two of those upon the south side totally dark, from the roof of the aisle being, by a modern innovation, carried *over* them. A cornice, elegant enough, but inappropriate, runs round the ceiling, which is itself neither elegant nor appropriate.

The oaken stalls are eighteen in number; the carved work is of the period of James the First, and is partially gilded.

At the lower end of the choir, a brass plate was until recently, nailed against the seat of the officiating minister, bearing the following anomalous inscription: "Here lieth William Smith, Bachelor in Divinity, and some time Schoolmaster and Fellow of Eton College, and *now* Viker of Sturminster Marshall, and Preacher of Winbourn, who died the 15 of Sept. A. D. 1587."

A marble, erected over one of the stalls to the memory of Mary, daughter of William Fitch, of High Hall, Esq. and wife of the Rev. William Russell, a minister of this church, who died Dec. 2, 1773, exhibits a beautiful epitaph from the pen of the Rev. John Derby, author of the account of Wimborne, in Mr. Hutchins' History of Dorset:

"Farewell, blest shade! from earth to heaven remov'd,
"In death lamented, as in life belov'd!
"Oh! if to bear a mild, a generous heart,

---

middle letter, was merely an abbreviation of the word JESUS, the Greek E bearing the figure of the English H, and the ancient Greek or Smyrnæn S, that of the english C. The Latins, however, interpreted it in their own characters to mean Jesus Hominum Consolator, or Salvator, and magnified the dash into a cross.

"To act the kindest, yet the firmest part;
"To fill each scene with decency and ease,
"In conscious merit ever sure to please;
"Prompt to relieve and to prevent distress,
"Feeling no greater blessing than to bless;
"To be whate'er or cheers or softens life,
"The tender parent, sister, friend, and wife;
"If, reader, these can claim a general tear,
"Approach, and pay the mournful tribute here."

The present organ, which ranks among the finest in the West of England, was originally erected in the year 1664, by the celebrated Father Schmidt, a German, who constructed that at the Temple Church, London; it was rebuilt, with additions, in 1764, and again underwent extensive improvements in 1844. It now comprises the following stops,* &c.

THREE ROWS OF KEYS.
GREAT ORGAN, CC, to F.

1 Open Diapason
2 Stop'd Diapason
3 Clarabella
4 Double Open Diap: Treb:
5 Double Open Diap: Bass
6 Principal
7 Twelfth
8 Fifteenth
9 Tierce
10 Larigot
11 Sesquialtera
12 Trumpet

SWELL ORGAN, Tenor, C to F; continued by Choir Organ Bass, to CC.

1 Open Diapason
2 Stop'd Diapason
3 Principal
4 Twelfth
5 Fifteenth
6 Oboe
7 Trumpet.

---

* This description of the Organ, as well as the list of Organists, has been kindly supplied by the present talented Organist, Mr. F. Blount, for this edition

CHOIR ORGAN, (detached) CC to F.

1 Stop'd Diapason   3 Fifteenth
2 Principal   4 Cremona

PEDALS.

CCC to E., 2 Octaves and a 3rd., large scale open diapason Copula movements.

1 Pedals to great organ   4 Choir to great organ
2 Pedals to choir organ   5 Swell to choir organ
3 Swell to great organ   6 Great to choir organ

COMPOSITION PEDALS.

1 Diapason   4 Trumpet
2 Full to Fifteenth   5 Full swell to Diapason
3 Full to Sesquialtera

The following is a list of the organists that have been appointed, from the reign of Queen Elizabeth to the present time, together with their salaries.

		£	s.	d.
1595	—— Maynard	16	0	0
	He was "Usher and Organiste."			
1609	Arthur Maynard	10	0	0
1611 to 1621	William Emes	12	0	0
1622	Thomas Noble	3	6	8
	"Organist and Singing Man."			
1625	—— Clum	12	0	0
1627 to 1638	—— Cottrell (Clerk and Org:)	12	0	0
1640 to 1644	—— Emes	12	0	0
"	In 1643	9	0	0
"	In 1644	6	0	0

(From 1645 to 1662 both inclusive, no Organist was appointed. This was the period of the Civil Wars with Cromwell, and includes also the whole time of his, and his son's Protectorate.)

		£	s.	d.
1663 to 1693 John Silver	22	0	0
In 1682 and thence till his death	24	0	0

(Previous to the advance of his salary, the Governors used generally to make him an annual present of £2; and for several years prior to his death, they paid his house rent. In 1696 they discharged the bill for his shroud, 6s., and for his coffin, 7s.)

1693 —— Henman	22	0	0
1694-5 to 1713 George Day	24	0	0
In 1701 till his death	25	0	0
1713 to 1742-3 John Fyler	25	0	0
1743 to 1765 George Coombes	25	0	0

(In 1765 he resigned, being chosen Organist at Bristol. His son succeeded him.)

1765 to 1798 Richard Coombes . . .	25	0	0

(Resigned from infirmities.)

1798 to 1808 William Mitchell	25	0	0
1808 to 1835 J. W. Blount	25	0	0
,, In 1818 . .	35	0	0
1835 F. S. Blount	40	0	0
,, In 1848, and now	80	0	0

We must not, however, omit to notice the elegantly-carved open doors within the pointed arches beyond the stalls, which tend so materially to ornament the choir, and with the curtains attached, to add to its comfort. The doors were imported from the Continent.

The cumbrous screen, erected in 1610, has been taken away, and the choir thereby thrown more open; the present mode of supporting the organ, namely, on two oak pillars, and a beam extending across the eastern arch of the tower, although in many respects preferrable to the former, has an appearance of insecurity, and does not convey a very pleasing effect to the eye. The four massive arches which support the tower, may be distinguished by the rudeness of their masonry, and the depth of mortar upon every layer of stone, as erections not long posterior to the Conquest. Over these, on either side, stand two pointed arches, each inclosing four round ones, with a carved head in the middle. The second story, which carries us above the height of the roof, we find is the reverse of what formed the lower compartment on the exterior; viz. two circular-headed windows, with a pointed arch, in outline only, between them. The third story is shut out by a panelled ceiled roof. A slender shaft, resting on a corbelhead, rises at each angle to the roof, except that in the N. W. which is terminated half way by a capital, supporting the turret staircase which connects the *triforia* with the upper portion of the tower.

We proceed a few paces into THE NAVE, now used as a parish church. The aisles are portioned off by six arches on either side, of which the four next the choir are pointed, but of early date, the first being smaller than the rest, and plain, the others profusely ornamented with billet mouldings, and resting upon round Norman piers, with corbels at the spring, and sculptured bosses, to resemble key-stones, at the juncture. A Norman cornice runs above in a straight line. The two further arches are of a later style, and supported by octagonal pillars. The *clerestory*, or upper tier of six windows, is still more modern, and very nearly square; divided into three dwarfish lights, and subdivided, near the top, into six. The former oaken roof, though probably but contemporary with the western tower, was yet a beautiful and ingenious specimen of carpentry, being fastened together with wooden pegs, without the help of nails, or any ligatures of iron. The present ceiled roof with its painted ribs and gilded bosses, present a gay contrast to other parts of the venerable structure.

The oaken pulpit was probably executed in the latter part of the reign of Queen Elizabeth. On the pavement beneath lies a stone, now covered under the flooring of a pew, but still retaining the pins to which were formerly, affixed a male and female figure in brass, supposed to have been those of John Herynge, Esq. and his wife, who died about the time of Henry the Seventh. The eagle, cast in 1623, is bold and handsome.

The great west window, with the gallery and stalls beneath, were completed under the superintendance of Mr. Evans, the county architect. This window opens to the belfry; its dimensions are extremely good, but the new mullions are of too perishable material to be considered a permanent feature in the building. Instead of common panes, *ground glass* has been substituted,—perhaps the best contrivance that could have been devised to obviate the error of building up a tower against the only window in the entire wall. The gallery is of deal, upheld by pillars of cast iron : and the pews below are of the same wood. The front of the gallery is panelled, with handsome oak carving ; this, as well as the carved doors in the choir, and the central part of the east window, was removed from some suppressed convents on the continent, and was also the gift of Mr. Bankes. Behind is preserved an old Lunar Orrery, on the Copernican system, which moves by the machinery of the clock, and shows in its monthly circuit round the dial-plate, the age and phases of the moon, the situation of the sun, and the revolutions of the earth, planets, tides, &c. There is another of the same kind in Exeter Cathedral, and a third in that of Wells.

The aisles, north and south of the nave, present little for observation. Each contains a porch-door, besides a range of five small windows with two lights. The old raftered roof is now ceiled, and has been so raised on either side, that a row of fair Norman windows above the arches of the nave, are rendered quite invisible. In the south aisle is preserved an old oak chest, or rather an oak tree, excavated like an Indian canoe, and formerly barricaded by six massive locks. Here were preserved the deeds and instruments of Joseph Collett's Charity, now deposited in the north aisle of the choir, secured after the same manner by six locks, the key to one of them being held by each of the six trustees.

The South TRANSEPT, to which we pass through a pointed arch, resting on marble shafts, may be very shortly dismissed. The window consists of five lights ; the modern transom is too high ; yet its details are far superior to that at the opposite extremity; where, however, we may observe on each side, a beautiful eliptical window, divided by a single mullion, and surmounted by a trefoil in a deep recess. This transept has been sometimes denominated *Death's Aisle*, from a strange painting of the King of Terrors bestriding his victim, with dart and spade in hand, and all the appropriate devices of mortality, which formerly covered the eastern wall, above the little niche in which are the remains of a piscina. By others it has been styled *Pope's Chapel*, from a dark tomb of brick, now concealed beneath the window, erected in 1663 to Elizabeth, Wife of Nicholas Pope. But in all probability the proper name was *Brembre's Chantry*: for near the middle of the floor lies the figure of an ecclesiastic, with short hanging sleeves, delicately carved in outline upon marble, which, from its perfect state, we may imagine had once been raised upon a monument. Over his head is a canopy, and at his feet a dog: on his right hand a spear, with a banner, charged with a cross between four crosslets; on his left another spear and banner, almost obliterated: but with the same arms repeated in the spandrils of the canopy. And here it is reasonably supposed that Thomas de Brembre, who died in 1361, lies interred. The figure is covered by the flooring. The roof is now ceiled, and a platform extends to the tower, the door and staircase to which are seen below. The gallery in each transept was erected under the direction of Mr. Evans, in 1836, and both are supported on cast iron pillars.

The CHOIR-AISLES are not coeval with the rest of the

church, and materially intrude upon the form of the cross. In the north, the roof has been lowered so much as to cut off a portion of the east window; in the south, it has been so much raised as to produce the same fault complained of in the aisles of the nave. The former of these is called *St. George's Chapel*, from a guild or fraternity of woollen manufacturers, who here performed devotions to their patron saint in the reigns of Henry the Seventh and Eighth. Near the large window reposes on a fragment of his tomb, the mutilated figure of a knight-templar, in his shield and coat of mail, with a lion under his head. Tradition assigns it either to one St. Piers, or to one Fitzherbert, Lords of Hinton Martel about six hundred years ago. The arms appear upon the shield, azure, three lions rampant, gules, in a bordure, engrailed. The monument of Mr. Joseph Collett, and his wife, who died about 1621, was rebuilt by his trustees in 1825. Towards the middle of this aisle are buried Henrietta Boston and Hannah Defoe, the two eldest daughters of Daniel Defoe, the noted Whig, and author of "The Adventures of Robinson Crusoe," who died in 1731, leaving a widow, son, and three daughters. From a brass plate belonging to an adjoining stone, but now deposited in a box in the Library, is copied the following inscription:

"O mortal man, before thy fatal fall,
"How, where, or when, thou knowest not at all:
"No sooner past thy wofull mother's wombe,
"But subject straighte unto the deserte tombe.
"Lyke that yow are, I lyved latelye here,
"Lyke that I am, you shortlye shall appere.

"From earthe I came, & soone to dust do yielde,
"All flesh must fade, as dothe the flower in felde.
"No state so sure, but deathe doth soone devowr;
"What then prevailes our pomp or puyssant power?
"Lyke as we fall, ryght so we ryse agayne,
"The just to joye, the rest to endlesse payne,
"Use then the tyme, so as when life doeth cease,
"Though corps consume, the soul may live in peace."
"Elenor Dickenson, passing to God, the xxiii of Sept. Anno Domini, 1571."

By an ample archway we hence descend eight steps into the crypt; formerly a subterraneous chapel, extending under the whole area of the chancel, and dedicated to the Virgin Mary. It was arched upon four large central columns and twelve others round the sides, with stone seats against the walls, and a piscina. In one of these arches on the north side, some antique fresco paintings have been lately discovered under the plaster. There was formerly an altar with images, an organ, and a pavement (some pieces of which were discovered by the present sexton, in 1839, whilst making a new vault beneath the stalls on the north side of the choir) of rich mosaic; these have all been long destroyed; and after remaining for many years under water, the principal space was apropriated by faculty as a private vault for the family of Mr. Bankes.

On the other side we ascend into the south aisle, which is chiefly conspicuous for the number of monuments it contains. At the eastern extremity of this aisle, Margaret, daughter of the Duke and Duchess of Somerset, who lie close by, founded and endowed a chantry. Near the centre of the pavement is a large grey slab without any traces of inscription, and lately levelled with the ground, but supposed to cover the remains of Dean Berwick, and now distinguished by a brass plate, inserted by the late Dr. Good, and inscribed: "Underneath lie the remains of John de Berwick, Dean of this Church; died 1312." Against the south wall is the monument of Thomas Hanham, of Dean's Court, Esq., and Margaret his wife, (1650). The kneeling figures are by no means contemptible, but the formal capitals and broken pediment betray the base architecture of the period. Beneath an arch in the wall, a few steps beyond, is a black marble coffin, partly raised above the ground, painted with coats of arms, guarded by iron railings; wherein are enshrined the ashes of Anthony Ettricke, of Holt Lodge, Esq., the first Recorder of Poole. This admirable lawyer and antiquary, but most eccentric gentlemen, grew towards his latter days, not only humoursome and phlegmatic, but so credulous of an impulse of the spirit, that, having once a share in some ship and cargo, which were announced to have safely reached the Portland Roads, he was still so far persuaded she would never gain the Port of London, as to sell his share in the property at a considerable discount. The good man's forebodings were verified; the ship and her cargo were lost. He now persuaded himself that his decease was fixed for the year 1691, and had this coffin made, and that date engraved upon it. The year, however, arrived and passed, and Mr. Ettricke was still alive. He therefore resolved to fix the coffin with his own hands; and having protested in an old fit of spleen against the people of Wimborne, that he would be buried neither in their church nor out of their church, neither above their ground nor below it, he obtained permission to evade the vow by placing it within the thickness of the wall, and on a level with the pavement. Here, in the year 1703, his remains were laid at last; and the sanctuary continues to be kept in repair by a fund of 20s. per annum, in trust with the Corporation of Poole. The original figures of the inscription can be plainly traced under the date afterwards written over them. Another monument of the same family is remarkable for an elegant inscription in Latin, attributed to the pen of Matthew Prior, whose birth-place has been often questioned, but who, there is very strong evidence to prove, was a native of Wimborne Minster. But the monument of Sir Edward Uvedale, erected by his wife, in 1606, is the stateliest in the whole collection. The entablature is supported by Corinthian pillars, under which the warrior in full armour lies stretched upon his side, his head resting upon his hand, which is raised upright from the elbow to the wrist: an effort of art worthy of a better age. The windows of this aisle are larger and handsomer than those on the north side of the choir, being similar in their divisions, though of shorter proportions, than that in the adjoining transept. An octagonal font, of Purbeck marble, stripped of its lead, but with traces of Norman decoration, has been removed hither, to make way for the gallery in the nave. Near the east window, in the south wall, a piscina has recently been brought to light; another has also lately been discovered under the east window of the north choir-aisle.

A little door now leads us through the vestry, the vaulted roof of which is worthy of a passing glance, up a winding staircase, into the library; a plain plastered room, formerly known as the Treasury, but converted to its present purpose in 1686. Some score volumes of moth-eaten divinity, the gift of the Rev. William Stone, slumber on the shelves, with their iron chains still dangling from the covers. There is also a cupboard full of ancient wills, deeds, and deed-baskets, and a curious old box in which offerings for the poor were formerly collected. The parochial registers commence in 1587. The following graphic sketch of the library having appeared in an interesting work, lately published,* we have, by the kind permission of the authoress, introduced it here.

'THERE is no sight that more powerfully carries back the thoughts to the olden time than an old library. I do not mean merely an old building, nor a collection of old books,—not a show-place, nor an elaborate modern antique,—but a veritable library of the olden time. There is a sight of this kind at the little town of Wimborne, in Dorsetshire. The old Minster of that place, bearing witness to the architectural skill and taste both of the Saxon and the Norman era, has much to delight the antiquarian in its structure, its ornaments, its traces of successive enlargements, marked by obvious changes of style, its monuments, and its historical associations. But nothing to my mind was so interesting as a chamber in one of the towers that was called "The Library." The room

---

* Sketches of English Literature, by Mrs. C. L. Balfour.

was square and well proportioned, though by no means large; two windows, of a sort of casement form, more suited to an old house than a church tower, and evidently very much more modern than the walls, admitted plenty of light; and round the two other sides of the room were rough-looking massive shelves, containing tarnished dilapidated books of all sorts, sizes, and colours, in clumsy but strong bindings, now sadly tattered, and in many cases dropping to pieces with age. Here were black-letter tomes — still older beautifully written manuscripts; specimens of early printing in the Roman character, that so soon triumphed over the black letter; a fine old polyglott Bible, in many volumes; and separate copies of the Scriptures — some in the original tongues, and some Latin, and early English translations.

The greatest peculiarity, however, was not the books, but the way they were secured. An iron rod went along the edge of each shelf, and was fastened at the end by a padlock. Each book had a chain screwed on to one of the covers (as we often see the Bible fastened to the desk in very old churches), and at the other end of the chain was a ring that ran on the locked iron rod. For the convenience of reading any of these venerable volumes thus guarded from removal, there was a portable desk and stool, which the reader could bring near any shelf, and, sitting sufficiently close for the chained book to rest upon the desk, he could peruse the volume there, and there only.

Nothing could appear more strange than the rusty iron chains hanging so thickly from the shelves — it seemed the prison rather than the home of the books. And this in olden times was the town library! It is probably that Wimborne was honoured above most towns of its size, not only by having its noble Minster, but by its possessing a public library of any kind. It is true that even from the early part of the sixteenth century it had a great advantage in its admirable school, which was founded by the illustrious Margaret Beaufort, the Mother of Henry VII., a woman who was deservedly called "the Mother of the Students of the Universities." And the probability is, that the townspeople, as books slowly increased, were tolerably competent to understand, and likely to value them.

There is a fine copy of Sir Walter Raleigh's "History of the World" in this old library, and local tradition attaches an interesting anecdote to this book. It is said the poet Prior used to read here often; and once when poring over the book in question on a winter evening, he fell asleep, and the candle, falling from the tin sconce of the desk upon the middle of the open book, burned slowly a round hole through it may be a hundred pages, rather more than less. The smoke of the smouldering paper aroused the weary student. A hand would have been sufficient to cover the damage and put out the fire, — and probably in this way it was extinguished. We may imagine, however, the dismay at the mischief done to a book, costly even now, but then of much higher monetary value. The pains taken to remedy the defect marks the value in which the book was held. Pieces of writing paper, about the size of half-a-crown, are very neatly pasted into the holes, and the words needed to supply the sense are transcribed from the memory, and, it is said, in the handwriting of Prior.

How strangely does this old library, with its rusty drapery of iron chains, hanging in dismal festoons from the shelves, contrast with the public libraries of the present time. And yet more remarkable, as a sign of intellectual progress, is the difference now in the price of books of the highest intrinsic value and importance. The chains are broken; the illustrious prisoners, so long fettered and kept from intercourse with the people, are free. They have spread over the land and multiplied, and found a welcome with high and low, rich and poor —

"Their thoughts in many a memory,
Their home in many a heart." '

In consequence of evening service having been recently appointed, gas has been introduced throughout the church, and, when lighted up, gives the exterior of the venerable structure, a very picturesque appearance.

In the CHURCH-YARD few epitaphs occur deserving a particular notice; we may take the following as some of the best specimens.

(West End) On James Kelham, died August 23, 1838, aged 39 years.

"A young man's life may well compared be,
"Unto the blossom of a fruitful tree;
"Which one day seems so pleasing, fair, and gay,
"And on the morrow fades and dies away:
"For this young man dropt in the midst of bloom,
"His days were spent, his sun did set at noon."

(North side.) On Richard Wareham, died January 19, 1827, aged 18 years.

"Ye thoughtless youths, be warn'd by me,
"My life was short as yours may be:
"Oh, prize the record God has giv'n,
"Repent, believe, and live for Heav'n!"

On Jane Pitman, died May 9, 1842, aged 78 years.

"Her life was humbly meekly spent,
"In courteousness and true content,
"Free from malice and of pride,
"So she liv'd and so she died."

On John Moors, died March 14, 1782, aged 58 years.

"O pious reader come draw near,
"And view the dust that lieth here;
"And when you read the fate of me,
"Think on the glass that runs for thee."

On George Hatchard, died June 30, 1821, aged 71 years.

"Come, gentle stranger, turn aside,
"Leave where thou art intrusive pride;
"On me this favour pray bestow,
"Approach and read these lines below.
"You're born in sin, estranged from God,
"And must be washed in Jesu's blood;
"Must know on earth your sins forgiven,
"If you expect to enter heaven.
"To this brief lecture pray attend,
"That's all—pass on obedient friend."

(South side.) On Elizabeth Strickland, died February 25, 1824, aged 47 years.

"Near Sudbury, in Suffolk, I was born,
"My years just forty-seven;
"And sudden from my husband torn,
"But hope to meet in Heaven.
"My children dear I left to mourn,
"When God did on me call,
"And if they do his will obey,
"He will reward them all."

(South side) On Mary Oakley, died August 18, 1764,
aged 55 years.

"Here rest a Woman good without pretence,
"Blest with plain reason and with sober sense,
"Passion and pride were to her soul unknown,
"Convinc'd that virtue only is our own."

On Melior Warne, died March 1, 1812, aged 26 years
and 9 months.

"Stop passenger and drop one pitying tear,
"O'er the lamented form that moulders here;
"Sad proof alas! how soon our bliss is flown,
"Joys but just tasted now for ever gone.
"Yet stay lov'd shade, ah! yet a moment stay,
"A moment and we all shall haste away,
"Thy Husband only waits thy child to rear,
"Sweet pledge of all on earth my soul holds dear;
"When she can spare me I will gladly come,
"Follow the summons to the silent tomb,
"Where we shall rest secure from mortal strife,
"Where none will wish to part the Man and Wife.

During the recent repairs and improvements, which have been carried out under the directions of the present churchwarden, and whilst forming a drain near the north-west porch, a curious old carved stone of Purbeck marble was discovered, having on one side a figure extended on the cross, and on the other side, one in an attitude of devotion; its original position has not yet been determined, it is now in the church under the care of the sexton.

The ALTARS of Wimborne Church were formerly no less than ten in number, all of them composed of alabaster and costly stones, and suitably garnished with plate and ornaments. Most of them had pictures or images of the saints, some of them in silver. To the high altar alone belonged a large cross of silver gilt; two plated crosses, with figures of silver; a foot and a staff, of copper, gilt; a plated cross, with image of copper; four silver candlesticks; two silver censers; a silver ship, or boat, for frankincense; a verger's rod, plated; six silver cruets; three paxes* and a gospel † of silver gilt; an oil-vat and six chalices, of the same; and twenty-four corporasses.‡ Also, an image of St. Cuthberge, with a ring of gold, and two little crosses of gold, with a book and staff in her hand; the head of the image in silver, with a crown of silver gilt; on her apron a St. James's shell, and a buckle of silver gilt. A cross in a case of silver gilt, and two hearts of gold hanging upon chains, plated at the back with silver. A pyx of silver. Two tabernacles of our Lady, one of gold with pearls, the other of silver gilt. A crucifix and two Agnus Dei's of gold. Besides a great many strings of beads, mostly coral, and set in silver; crucifixes, and other properties of inferior metal.

Its (asserted) RELICS were in no wise inferior to its wealth; these amounted to upwards of fifty, and included,—

A piece of the cross.

Part of our Lord's robe.

A large stone from His sepulchre.

A piece of the altar upon which our Lord was lifted up, and offered, by Simeon.

Some hairs of our Lord's beard.

---

* Small Crucifixes, on which the "kiss of peace" was given.
† A shrine, or box, in which the host was lifted up.
‡ Communion-cloths.

35

A part of the clothes in which Simeon wrapped our Lord when he offered Him in the temple.

A piece of the pillar, to which our Lord was bound and scourged.

Some of the ground where He was born.

A piece of the alabaster box.

One of the shoes of St. William.

Part of the thigh of the Virgin Agatha.

Some bones of St. Catharine.

Part of St. Mary, the Egyptian.

Part of the robe from our Lord's sepulchre.

Part of our Lord's manger.

A thorn from His crown.

One of St. Philip's teeth.

Some blood of St. Thomas a Becket.

One of the stones wherewith St. Stephen was martyred

The hair shirt of St. Francis.

Part of the cord that bound the thighs of St. Anthony.

&c., &c., &c.

THE CHURCH has continued to this day a Royal Peculiar, though not exactly independent of episcopal jurisdiction. Cathedral service is performed on Sundays, and every Thursday evening, and morning prayers every day by three clergymen in turn, nominated and paid at discretion, with the other stipendiaries of the school and church, by the Corporation, in accordance with the new scheme hereafter referred to, and which provides for the administration of the Charity and the distribution of the ample income, vested in the Corporation. It is to be regretted that this noble charity,—in common with many others throughout the country—has suffered extensively in its resources. For many years, and up to a very recent period, the annual sum *collected*, amounted to little more than one-third of the present income; in addition to which—a large sum having subsequently accumulated from the improved revenue—legal expenses diverted a considerable part of the funds which would otherwise have been available for the purposes of the charity, and the carrying out of the benevolent intentions of the founders. The present income of the Corporation is in a flourishing condition, and is applied in accomplishing the purposes of the scheme, as the means of doing so are furnished.

One of the above ministers has usually acted as the Official; but that honor is at present held by the Rev. E. Bankes. Of the three chapelries—Leigh, Kingston Lacey, and Holt—once annexed to the Minster, the latter alone has been preserved for purposes of public worship, and was rebuilt a few years since. The only prebendal house which remained standing in 1849, was taken down, and its site thrown into the new school premises.

THE FREE SCHOOL stands toward the southern extremity of the town. It was originally founded by Margaret, Countess of Richmond and Derby, only daughter of John Beaufort, Duke of Somerset, before alluded to, in the first year of King Henry the Eighth (1509); but having fallen into decay at the dissolution, it was re-instituted, in 1562, by Queen Elizabeth, for the instruction of "all her subjects' sons in learning, good manners, and virtue, according to the customs of Winchester and Eton." The school, and schoolmaster's house, as well as the houses for the priests, were also granted by the Queen; but the governors were bound to find a master, three priests, and their clerks, and to repair the chancel of the Minster, and the priests' houses, for ever. (It was about this time that divine service was discontinued at St. Peter's Chapel, Kingston, and a Friday's Lecture established in its place at Holt. The last person who held this office was a Covenanter—(few offices are held *after* a Covenanter)—one Constant Jessop, who in 1652, undertook the entire duty of the church, and performed none of it.)

Towards the close of the same century the school-house was rebuilt, at the expense of the governors, and under the direction of Thomas Hanham, Esq. serjeant at law; as appeared from his arms, and the remains of an inscription in one of the chamber windows:

"HOC PERFECIT
OPUS, SUA CURA,
THOMAS HANHAM,
SERVIENS AD LEGEM;
UT QUÆ FORTUNÆ," &c.

It has since been partially destroyed by fire, and again re-constructed. It was taken down in the year 1849, to make room for the present enlarged and handsome structure. Till within the last sixty or seventy years, the respectable diversion of cock-fighting is said to have been maintained with peculiar zeal, on Shrove Tuesday, among the students of Queen Elizabeth's Grammar School.

The present school-house is erected in the Tudor style of architecture, from the designs of Morris and Hebson;

the corner-stone was laid by the Lord Bishop of Salisbury, in November, 1849. The building embraces two large schools, small library, muniment-room, offices, and houses for the head and under masters; the materials used in the erection, are bright red brick, diapered with blue; Caen and Purbeck stone dressings; and covered with tiles and slate. From the western entrance to the town, it presents a pleasing feature, as well as from other spots in the neighbourhood.

For the due administration of the affairs of the charity, the regulation of the School, the appointment and salaries of the masters, the payment of the three ministers and clerks, as well as the organist, and choristers, a new SCHEME was prepared, and received the confirmation of the high Court of Chancery, on the 3rd. of June, 1848. It was also ordered to be "printed, and a copy given to every Governor of the charity, and to every person who may hereafter become a Governor, and every Priest, Master, Under Master, and Usher, or other person appointed under the said Charter or under the provisions of this Scheme, shall, on accepting and before entering on the duties of his office, by writing signed by him at the foot of one of such printed copies of this Scheme, certify that he has read the same, and that he undertakes and agrees to conform to and comply with, and be bound by, the provisions thereof, so far as the same apply to the office accepted by him." This Scheme directs to be spent, "a sum not exceeding £4500, as the Master to whom this cause stands referred shall find to be necessary, for the purpose of substantially repairing and fitting up, or rebuilding the present school-house and school premises, or for the purchase of a new school site, and building a new and enlarged School-house, and for purchasing or repairing, or building premises for occupation and use by the masters and scholars of the said School; such purchases, repairs, or new buildings to be according to a plan or scheme to be approved of by the said Master." This sum, however, was found inadequate to complete the present extensive building, which was erected at a cost of about £6000. A second sum to the amount of £3500, is directed to be set apart "for the purpose of repairing the chancel of the church;" and a third sum amounting to £1500, for the purchase of "a site for, and erecting in a convenient spot within the district of Holt, part of the parish of Wimborne, a house for the residence of one of the priests." These two last-named provisions yet remain to be carried out, want of funds having for a time suspended their execution.

The instruction afforded in this royal foundation-school, comprises the "Greek, Latin, and French languages, Mathematics, Arithmetic, General English Literature and Composition, Sacred and Profane History, Geography, Reading and Writing;" and "all boys of eight years and upwards, being English subjects, and able to read and write, and being certified to be of good moral conduct, and not being the subject of any infectious disease, shall, to the extent of the capacity of the school to accommodate them, be capable of admission to the said school, and to partake of all the benefits and advantages thereof; subject however, in case they require instruction *other* than in Latin and Greek, to the payment of the sum of £3, as and for the yearly payment for the additional branches of instruction in the said school other than Latin and Greek ;" and " that any boy who shall be desirous of learning Latin and Greek only, shall be taught and instructed in the Latin and Greek languages free of charge." " That all printed books required for or used by the scholars in the said school shall be provided by and at the expense of the parents or relatives of the said scholars respectively, but that all paper, pens, ink, pencils, and other stationery necessary for the use of the scholars in the said school shall be provided and found by and out of the fund received from scholars, or out of the general income of the said Charity, as the said Governors may from time to time appoint."

"That there shall be at least one annual Examination of the Boys at the said School, the period of which Examination shall be fixed by the Governors, and such examination shall take place in the presence of the said Governors, or such of them as can conveniently attend, and of the Masters of the said School, and of such other persons as the said Governors may from time to time think fit to invite to attend the same." " That the said Governors may, after every such Examination, distribute such and so many prizes (the value of such prizes not to exceed in any one year £25) as they may think fit to and among the meritorious Scholars educated in the said School, who shall distinguish themselves for learning or good conduct, and who in the judgment of the Head Master of the said School and the Governors, shall be most deserving of the same, and the expences of and attending such Examination and the said prizes shall be defrayed and paid by the Governors out of the Annual Income of the said Charity."

"That the sum of £100 be applied by the said Governors towards the founding of a Library of Books, combining useful and entertaining knowledge for the improvement and recreation of the boys, to be called 'the School Library.' Such Library to be established by the Governors, and to be under the control and management of the Head Master, and that the sum of £10 be annually applied towards the support and increase thereof out of the income of the said Charity."

"That the Master and Under Master shall be at liberty to receive into their respective houses as boarders, such number of boys, for education in the said school, as the Governors shall from time to time in writing authorise them to receive, provided that the number of boarders so taken by the said Master does not at any time exceed thirty, and by the Under Master fifteen in the whole."

For the performance of the duties connected with the Minster and School, the Governors have to provide three Clergymen, an Organist, four Clerks (including one for Holt), three Singing Men, six Choristers; Head Master, Under Master, a Master to intruct in the English Language, Writing, Arithmetic Geography, &c., and a Master in Foreign Languages; all of whom are appointed and paid by the Corporation.

The INDEPENDENT CHAPEL is situated near the northern entrance to the town, and is built in the pointed gothic style of architecture, it was erected in the year 1846, and contains between four and five hundred sittings; this chapel cost about £700, nearly the whole of which was raised by the efforts of the church and congregation assembling there; it is—like many other public buildings—greatly deficient in ventilation, and from this cause, and its open roof being slated, a great degree of heat in the summer, and cold in the winter is experienced. The history of the congregational church, dates nearly two hundred years back; the following is an abridged account of the same, as recorded by a late respected minister* who held the office of pastor for more than twenty years. The first minister who laboured here was the Rev. Thomas Rowe, M.A., of Exeter College, Oxford; who commenced preaching at Little Canford, in his own house, "to a crowded congregation collected from all the surrounding country, receiving no remuneration, excepting in the last half year, when the rent of his house was paid. During this time he preached occasionally at Wimborne in the yard of the late Mr. George Oakley, hosier; in a building on the site of which a wool warehouse has since been erected, near the premises of Mr. Fryer; in the house contiguous to the Baptist Meeting, where his successor sometimes resided, and probably himself; and in the more dangerous periods, he preached at Ashley Wood, in the neighbourhood."

"In 1672, a meeting house was built, and he resided at

---

* Author of "Pharaoh" a Poem.

Wimborne till his death, which took place, Oct. 6, 1680. He was buried at Lytchett, and his funeral sermon was preached there by his intimate friend, the Rev. S. Hardy, of Poole. A flat stone before the rails of the altar bears an inscription to his memory. Palmer, in his Nonconformist's Memorial, speaks of him in the following terms. 'Mr. Rowe was a very humble, serious man, and a close walker with God; a strict observer of the Lord's day, and a daily practitioner in the art of divine meditation. Prayer was his delight and constant exercise. He was a close reprover of sin wherever he saw it, even though he expected the warmest resentment : and God often rewarded his fidelity by making the event quite different.' 'He was entirely satisfied in his nonconformity, and had so great a value for the ministry in that way, under all its discouragements, that he always designed, and solemnly devoted his eldest son to it from the womb. God carried him through all his service and difficulties with great cheerfulness and satisfaction : and he took notice how mercifully God provided for him as to this world, in making the little he had in it go farther, and afford him truer pleasure after his ejectment, than a much larger income before.'"

"For half a century after the death of Mr. Rowe the succession of ministers cannot be correctly ascertained. The first meeting-house, which was also the first place of dissenting worship in this part of the country, was frequently attended by the Earl of Shaftesbury, author of the Characteristics ; and by Sir John Trenchard, Chancellor of the Exchequer in the reign of William III.

Lady Trenchard appears to have been an eminently pious woman. She attended sometimes the meeting-house at Wimborne, sometimes that of Bere-Regis, till she died."

"There was at this early period a large manufactory of shalloons in Wimborne. This was carried on at the west side of the town, occupying the whole of the field now called Redcotts. The masters and all the workmen were dissenters. By some persons in authority a fine of a shilling a head was imposed on those who did not attend the parish church, which being afterwards increased, caused the removal of the manufactory from the town. The congregational church at Wimborne is rendered farther interesting as being the home of two daughters of Daniel Defoe, (already referred to) who were its members."

"In Nov. 1695, the site of the late meeting-house was assigned by Mary and Christabella Corne to trustees, for the use of dissenters. The names of the first trustees are John Clifford, John Smith, John Reeks, Richard Wright, and Thomas Moren. Probably the minister who succeeded Mr. Rowe was Mr. Benson, who had Mr. Webb for his assistant. The Rev. John Greene was ordained, July 20, 1708, and his ordination sermon, by Theophilus Lobb, of Shaftesbury, is in print. To him probably succeeded the Rev. Miles Baxter, He was at Wimborne in 1721, when he was left one of the trustees to a charity which still exists. He was in 1745 resident at Westbury, Somerset. The Rev. John Farmer was also a minister of this church, the author of a volume of sermons, and some time pastor of the dissenting church at Needham Market, Suffolk. In 1738 died James Clarke, gardener, leaving a garden for the maintenance of the minister; and £3. to purchase a book of martyrs, to be chained in some convenient place in the meeting. In the year 1756 the Rev. John Punphill took the charge of the congregation, which remained under his care till 1767, when he removed to Birmingham. To him succeeded the Rev. Samuel Badcock, who was ordained August the 29th, 1769. A very considerable attention was excited in the town by his preaching. In 1771 an application being made to Dr. Conder, of Homerton, Mr. Jameson, one of the students, visited Wimborne, and continued till the beginning of the year 1772. In the year 1774. Mr. Panton was ordained. This gentleman, who had recently left the Countess of Huntingdon's College, was a young man of great piety, of amiable manners, and of respectable, but not striking talents. His literary acquirements were of a very humble order. He was however, likely to have been useful, for he took pains to instruct the young people of his congregation; but he died on the 30th of March, 1778, aged only 27 years. A marble tablet in the chapel records his name and virtues. He left a widow, who was afterwards married to Dr. Duncan, his successor, and who till very lately, survived them both. In December, 1778, Mr. Holmes preached on probation, and on April 15th, 1779, he accepted an invitation to become the pastor of the church, over which he continued till about Midsummer 1782. His immediate successor was Mr., afterwards Dr., Duncan, who accepted the call of the church in October, 1782, and came to live at Wimborne in the following year. During Mr. Duncan's residence here his wife died, and he married the widow of Mr. Panton. While residing in this place he received a diploma, creating him Doctor in Divinity, which is said to have been procured for him by Mr. Pitt, in return for some political communication made by Mr. Duncan to the Premier. The congregation was probably, as flourishing during Dr. Duncan's ministry, as at any period of its history since the time of Mr. Rowe. In the year 1788, the late meeting-house was built, about which time the secession of some members originated a small Baptist congregation, which continued for a long series of years under the faithful ministry of the Rev. John Miell. The Rev. Mr. Foxell came to reside at Wimborne about Midsummer, 1800, and left in March, 1804. In December of the same year, the Rev. Mr. Ralph became pastor of the church, and remained till January, 1811. After him the Rev. Alexander Good preached twenty Sabbaths, very much to the gratification of the people. The Rev. Wm. Miles came to Wimborne, at Midsummer, 1812, and was ordained the 27th of July, 1814. He continued here till September 28, 1819. On the 31st. of October, the Rev. J. O. Stokes came on probation, and on the 14th. of January, 1820, settled at Wimborne, where he staid till June 3, 1824. On June 12th, the Rev. Samuel Spink, of North Tawton, Devonshire, came on probation, and undertook the pastoral duties, August 25th. of the same year." He remained for a period of about twenty years, and was distinguished for his literary attainments and love of study, by which he gained the attention and respect of many in the town who did not regularly attend his preaching. During his ministry the congregation was much increased, and in 1829 the meeting-house was enlarged, and a school-room built. He removed in 1844. In 1845, the Rev. I. Brown was ordained, and continued till 1846, when he removed. He was greatly instrumental in the erection of the present chapel, already mentioned, which was built during his ministry, and opened in 1846, by the Rev. Dr. Harris. The Rev. Theophilus Flower succeeded him, and took the charge of the congregation in 1848, but removed to Wells in the year 1853.

The WESLEYAN CHAPEL stands in the corn market, and is a commodious building with ample accommodation for its sabbath school, as well as convenient vestries. It was originally built in 1820, but considerably enlarged in 1843, and again remodelled in 1846. It has galleries round three of its sides, in the front one of which stands the organ. It is lighted with gas, and contains between four and five hundred sittings.

The NATIONAL SCHOOL is situated in king's street, and consists of two large rooms, and lobbies; one of the rooms being occupied by the boys, and the other by the girls attending the school; attached is a spacious play ground fenced in the front and divided in the middle with strong, but light iron railings; the partition between the rooms is so constructed as to be easily removed, to form one large room when required, for public religious meetings, concerts, &c. The school was erected in 1843. A bazaar in aid of the funds of this as well as the school at Holt, was held at Merley House and realized a handsome amount.

The BRITISH SCHOOL is conducted in the school-room on the premises of the Independent chapel, and numbers at present, under one hundred scholars.

The MECHANICS' INSTITUTION was established in 1836, and is now in a flourishing condition, its members averaging above one hundred ; the annual subscription—which is only five shillings—is much below that of neighbouring similar institutions, but by the assistance of those desirous of promoting the interests of the institution, not only have lectures in the various sciences, and others of an instructive character been delivered, but the library has been also increased yearly, and now numbers many hundred volumes. The meetings of the institution are held, and the lectures delivered in the NEW TOWN HALL, a building erected by private enterprise, in church street ; in which many of the public meetings in the town are held, The hall, though recently built, is not found to meet all the requirements of the town, and needs enlarging.

ST. MARGARET'S HOSPITAL, originally designed for lepers, and an endowment of exceedingly remote antiquity, stands about a quarter of a mile upon the road, north-west of Wimborne. The date of its establishment, though deeds are still preserved relating to it so far back as the reign of King John, has long continued entirely unknown. It seems not unlikely that the asylum was repaired and enlarged either by John of Gaunt, or by some other of the family of Lancaster before the year 1400. Its total revenues were returned, in 1786, at £60. 9s. having been augmented by several bequests, particularly that of Dr. Stone, Principal of New Inn Hall, Oxford, in 1685. A dozen alms-people are now constantly on the books, being nominated, of course without the intended qualification, by the Lords and Steward of the Manor of Kingston Lacey. The chapel, though ruinous, is extremely picturesque, and not without value to the eye of a connoisseur.

THE MARCHIONESS OF EXETER'S ALMS-HOUSES, six in number, stand near the entrance of the town from the Ringwood road. They were founded by bequest of the Lady Gertrude Courtenay, in 1557, for six poor men and women, who continue to be appointed and paid by the Lord of the Manor of Canford.

Such are the principal foundations of charity in the town of Wimborne Minster; and when taken with the subjoined catalogue of minor donations, they present an amount, which, if fully kept up according to their original institutions would be exceeded in few places of the like population in England.

BOXLEY'S GIFT. Thomas Boxley, of this parish, gentleman, gave by will, dated 1561, a moiety of Rushly Meadow, value at this time £5 per annum, one half to the poor, and the other half to public works in the parish; and an acre of land in Rowlands, to St. Margaret's Hospital.

GUNDRY'S GIFT. Mary Gundry, of this town, widow, by will dated 1617, gave, besides a house to the service of the church, the sum of 40s. per annum to the poor.

LYNE's GIFT. Thomas Lyne, of Bradford Bryant, in this parish, by will dated 1621, gave, among other charities 40s. a year to the poor; and £6 per annum towards the education of a poor scholar at Oxford or Cambridge, to be taken, every third or fourth year, out of the free-school at Ringwood, or for want of a boy competent to go from thence, out of the schools of Wimborne or Sherborne.

COLLETT's GIFT. Joseph Collett, of this place, gentleman, by deed dated 1621, settled divers lands and tenements in the Borough of Corfe Castle, yielding rent £20. 15s. per annum, to five poor men and five poor women of this parish.

BROWNE's GIFT. Alice Browne, of Wimborne, by will dated 1637, devised to the poor of the town an annuity of 20s. which is now, with a similar donation from her executor Gundry Brown, vested in a barn in west street.

HABGOOD's GIFT. Richard Habgood, of Wimborne, tanner, settled, in 1642, certain messuages, for the relief of the parochial poor, amounting, with a donation from his daughter, Edith Hall, (1683,) to about £20 per annum.

MITCHELL's GIFT. Bernard Mitchell, of Weymouth, merchant, by will dated 1646, bequeathed to the poor of Wimborne the sum of 20s. per annum in trust of the churchwardens.

GILLINGHAM's GIFT, Roger Gillingham, of the Middle Temple, London, Esq., by will dated 1695, founded a school and alms-house at Pamphill, in this parish, for a schoolmaster, four men, and four women, (none married, nor under the age of 55) to be nominated by the Governors of Queen Elizabeth's school; and forty poor scholars. The endowment amounts to £65 per annum. The same person also bequeathed the sum of £200, to be lent out, in sums of £5, for terms not exceeding four years, on good security to poor tradesman; but this bequest, owing to the poverty of the affairs of the deceased was never paid.

COSTIN'S GIFT. John Costin, a native of Scotland, afterwards a mercer of Wimborne, by will dated 1721, devised two parcels of land, producing about £8 per annum, towards the support of four poor tradesmen in the town.

THE TOWN of Wimborne Minster is built with more attention to convenience than regularity. It comprises about 476 houses, and 1896 inhabitants; is governed by two bailiffs, and, though never actually incorporated, is dignified with the title of a Borough. The houses are mostly neat, and the roads clean and good. There are two Banks in the town; one a branch of the Wilts and Dorset Banking Company, in the Square; the other, a branch of the National Provincial Bank of England, in the west borough. Within the suburbs and environs are no less than five BRIDGES. Two of these, Isebrook, or Eastbrook Bridges, cross the two branches of the river Allen; Walford bridge crosses the same river on the northern road; Julien Bridge (a very noble structure, so called after Walter Julien, its supposed architect) crosses the Stour upon the road to Corfe Mullen; this bridge has been lately widened and extensively repaired under the direction of the county Architect, Mr. Evans, on whom its picturesque and handsome appearance reflects great credit. Canford Bridge, crosses the same river on the Roman road to Poole. The only trade now carried on, that of knit stockings, is of very humble pretensions; its manufactures of linen and woollen have fallen into disuse since the days of Charles the Second. The market once held throughout Sunday and Monday, is now transferred to Friday. A cattle-fair, which was also held on Good Friday, was changed, in 1765, to the Friday preceding, and there is another for general traffic, on the 14th September. The population of the entire parish, according to the census of 1821, was 3563; in 1851, it amounted to 4756.

The principal object of curiosity in the neighbourhood is the celebrated encampment of BADBURY RINGS, in the parish of Shapwick, before adverted to, which occupies the summit of a considerable eminence, and commands a view over many miles of country. The camp is circular, about a mile in circumference, with treble ramparts and ditches, and two entrances, one opening, on the north-east, upon the Roman Road to Old Sarum, a second, south-west, towards Dorchester; besides a third in the outer rampart only, diverging towards Blandford. Camden supposes it a Saxon work; Mr. King a British; the more usual opinion assigns it to the Romans, though it was probably only occupied, and not constructed, by that people. A Roman sword, with urns, coins, and other reliques, was dug up in 1665.

The town enjoys the advantage of railway communication; the South-Western Railway from London to Dorchester, running within half a mile of it; the Station is about three quarters of a mile south-east of the town. A single line of rails only, is at present laid down between Dorchester and Southampton, as it is however, in contemplation to extend the line westward from Dorchester to Exeter, it is intended to make a double line of rails from Dorchester to Southampton. It is worthy of remark, that the line has been hitherto peculiarly exempt from serious accidents.

The NUNNERY at Stapehill, is about three miles from the town, and is a Roman Catholic establishment of the order of La Trappe; the chapel, which has been lately built, is a neat structure with a small spire, and can be seen from a considerable distance. It is to be regretted that these establishments in this country are not subject to some kind of inspection or periodical visitation, which would not only prevent unwilling detention or other abuse —if such exists—but effectually remove all suspicion of the same, if the contrary were found to be the case. It is occasionally that the frightened and timid nun is seen in the town, pursuing her flight from her unnatural—and we may add unscriptural—seclusion, dreading nothing so much as recapture and a return to the rigour of conventual life.

  *   *   *   *   " that she might avoid
 " A rigid cloister-life, she had employed,
 " When all her earnest pleadings had been vain,
 " A stratagem her liberty to gain."

  *   *   *   *   *   *

 " Within a convent he would place his child,
  *   *   " The fatal day arrives, and Rosalie
 " Must bid Adieu! to all, save Memory!

"Yes, every hope, and every tender thought
"Must now be banished, or at least be taught
"To sleep in silence; oh! 'tis sad to think,
"One moment's vows can break each cherished link.
"Hush! hush! a choir of Sisters chaunt the song,
"Which tells, that now amongst the busy throng
"There is a maiden, a young, pensive one,
"Who is approaching to be veiled a nun;
"Their dulcet tones all mingle in the air,
"As if Euterpe's self were warbling there.
"But see, the Priests their victim lead along,
"Who does not seem as though she heard the song;
"In robes of Innocence the maid is clad,
"But oh! how pale, disconsolate, and sad!
"Her silken tresses down her shoulders wave,
"And rarest treasures of Peru's rich cave
"In wreaths around each snowy arm are bound,
"A brilliant, jewelled coronal is round
"The hapless victim's unresisting head,
"And thus attired, the drooping Rose is led,
"Like her fair namesake, when a summer shower
"Has decked with liquid pearls the tender flower;
"Thus she advances, or is slowly led,
"To take her station on the lowly bed,
"Where she, in all her splendour, is to lie,
"And, strewed with flowers, is from the world to die.

There are also several COUNTRY SEATS, within a short distance of Wimborne, particularly deserving of attention.

KINGSTON LACY, the seat of the Right Hon. George Bankes, M.P., near Badbury Rings, was erected by Sir Ralph Bankes, in 1663. Besides a commodious library, there is an extensive and elegant saloon, enriched with a most valuable collection of paintings by Caracci, Salvator Rosa, Murillo, Berghem, Vandyke, Sir Godfrey Kneller, Sir Peter Lely, and other eminent masters. In the park is also erected a remarkable Egyptian Obelisk, brought over by a brother of the above gentleman, from the island of Philæ: the first stone of the base to support it was laid by the late Duke of Wellington, in 1827. James, Duke of Ormond, was so delighted with a temporary visit to this house, that he spent the latter portion of his life, and died, in it, anno 1688.

GAUNT's HOUSE, about three miles north, on the Salisbury road, near Honeybrooke, is also assigned to the great Duke of Lancaster, and still retains symptoms of its ancient moat: it is now the property and country seat of Sir Richard Plumtre Glynn, Bart.

HIGH HALL, about two miles north-west, the property and seat of Benjamin Linthorne, Esq., formerly belonged to the family of Gilly, as well as that of the Tregonwells, of Milton Abbas. Though not extensive, it is elegant, and delightfully situated.

MERLEY HOUSE, remarkable for the sumptuous room designed and constructed by Ralph Willet, Esq., for the reception of his magnificent library; the house, though pleasantly situated on an eminence overlooking the town, and standing in a good park, in which there is a well-stocked fish pond, is at present unoccupied.

CHARBOROUGH, the ancient seat of the families of Earl and Drax, is celebrated as the spot on which the "Glorious Revolution" was first planned, in 1686, by Earle Drax, Esq., with King William and his associates; a circumstance testified by an inscription erected in 1780, over the entrance to a subterraneous apartment in the grounds, now used as an ice-house. A family chapel is also attached to the residence. Distance from Wimborne, about six miles, west; the property of John Samuel Wanley Sawbridge Erle Drax, Esq.

HENBURY HOUSE, occupied by George Harris, Esq., is pleasantly situated near Corfe Mullen, about three miles and a half west of the town.

LOWER HENBURY, the property of Charles Parke, Esq., stands about half a mile beyond Henbury House, its park extending for some distance along the new turnpike road leading from Wimborne to Dorchester, through Piddletown.

KNOWLE COTTAGE, the residence of W. C. Lambert, Esq., also adjoining Henbury House and Park, is a good house, and situated on a beautiful declivity, it enjoys extensive views.

UDDENS HOUSE, the property of Edward Greathead, Esq., now rented by G. T. Sullivan, Esq. The house is pleasantly situated about three miles on the Ringwood road, and the wooded grounds around it form a pleasant contrast with the barren heath beyond.

STONE COTTAGE, the seat of Rear Admiral Garland, stands in a pretty, though small park, about three quarters of a mile from the town; it is situated on a hill, and whilst it is backed by some fine timber, the front is open, and affords a good prospect of the town, together with the river Stour and its meadows.

FARRS COTTAGE, the residence of Mrs. H. Garland Müller, is pleasantly situated on the side of a hill, about a mile north-west of the town.

CANFORD HOUSE, the property and occasional residence of Lady Charlotte Guest, was purchased by the late Sir J. Guest, M.P., of the Right Hon. Lord de Mauley. It was for some time occupied as a Convent for Ursulines, and distinguished for the large and curious kitchen of John of Gaunt, attached and over part of which are two rooms or chambers, the ascent to which is matter of speculation, as no traces are now to be discovered of any stairs or steps leading to the same. The house was rebuilt by his Lordship (at that time the Hon. W. Ponsonby), under the superintendance of Mr. Edward Blore, in a style of magnificence, imitative of the noblest architecture of Queen Elizabeth. It was the residence for nearly twelvemonths, of the late Queen Dowager, who expressed much satisfaction with the house and grounds. It was again extensively enlarged and much improved by the late Sir J. Guest, who added the Victoria tower, which is built on two arches and affords a carriage drive under, which now constitutes the grand entrance, and is an object, which from its height attracts notice from a considerable distance, whilst the architecture and carving are of the highest and best style.

But whilst there is much to admire in the house itself, the greatest attraction and the objects of the most intense interest we think will be, those relics of by-gone ages, the monuments of a great people, the eloquent though silent historians and witnesses of a powerful empire long since swept away, glimpses of whose history we have seen in that unerring and oldest record in the world—the Bible. The enquiry has been made, why do we not find more mention made in the Scriptures of such an extensive Empire? and we think it satisfactorily answered, namely, that the Bible is a history of God's people, and only mentions others when brought into contact with them. THE NINEVEH MARBLES, with which the house is enriched, were excavated and brought to this country by the indefatigable exertions of Mr. Layard, they were obtained by great labour, and transported over a wide extent of country with much difficulty, and were floated down rivers, when available, on air bags. They are however, of such importance, on various grounds, as far to exceed in value, all the labour and exertions required to obtain and convey them to this country. A suitable building has been erected for the reception of these marbles, connected with the house by cloisters, or, a corridor, neither of which is yet completed; the tapestry and furniture coverings will be in unique colours, and such as have been discovered by Mr. Layard to have been in use in the palaces from whence the marbles were taken; these adornments are in progress, and will be the result of the skill and taste of Lady C. Guest herself. The Sculptures—some of which are already fixed—will be arranged in panels round the walls, and facing the entrance. The most conspicuous objects which present themselves on entering are a colossal Bull, on the right hand, and colossal Lion on the left; each with a human head, and winged; to both of which there is the peculiarity of possessing five legs, which permits a front view shewing the fore legs and chest, whilst a side view shews four legs of each animal, which is represented walking. On these, and indeed most of the Sculptures, there are elaborate inscriptions, running in long straight lines. Nor are these inscriptions altogether unintelligible, as many remarkable discoveries have been made relative to individuals. In the course of the research instituted amongst these ruins of Assyrian grandeur, a representation of Sennacherib himself was found seated, and surrounded by his officers, with the following inscription above his head:

"Sennacherib, the mighty King, King of the country of Assyria, sitteth on the throne of judgment before the city of Lachish. I give permission for its slaughter."

The name of Hezekiah himself has been discovered in some inscriptions as well as that of Sennacherib, Jehu, Omri, and many others. Mr. Layard discovered the Record Chamber of a palace, in which many clay seals attached to the records were still remaining. Some of these seals are Egyptian, having been attached to treaties entered into with the Egyptian Pharaohs. One of the seals contained two inscriptions; the one being that of the King of Assyria, the other that of the King of Egypt, both on the same lump of clay, affording one of the most striking tokens of amity and concord that history furnishes.

The Sculptures deposited here represent various scenes and events, some of them apparent and easily understood, others less so and difficult of interpretation, but all give evidence of a great advance in art, and impress the mind of the beholder with awe; not so much the effect of the sculptures themselves as the wonderful manner in which they have been preserved during so many ages, and the enduring and so long hidden history of the people they represent, and most of all from the new species of evidence for the truths of revelation which they afford. Some of the Slabs—which are all carved in relief—represent emblems of idolatry,—their God Nisroch, the tree of life, with kneeling priests, a priest in sacerdotals; others, a king in his robes, with attendant eunuchs; male and female figures; captives, warriors, &c. Some will no doubt recognise in the representations of the captives, the features peculiar to the Jewish race. It is worthy of remark, that whilst these marbles are nearly the only remains of a great empire, the Jews, though scattered, retain their distinctive characteristics intact, and, can we doubt it, are preserved for a triumphant return to their own land,—when the veil of unbelief is removed—again to become an influential nation.

The only NATIVES of Wimborne, celebrated in the annals of her chroniclers, are Matthew Prior, the Poet, who notwithstanding some obscurity in the circumstances of his birth, was in all probability born of humble parents in this town, in the year 1664; and Matthew Gill, a natural phenomenon, who died in 1767, and of whom a description may be found in any Guide to the County of Dorset.

THE END.

Purkis, Typ., Wimborne.

Milton Keynes UK
Ingram Content Group UK Ltd.
UKHW051504171123
432728UK00004BA/93